DROP BY DROP

To my grandson, Nathan Max
–J. J.

To my husband Andrey
–Y. N.

KAR-BEN PUBLISHING, INC.
A division of Lerner Publishing Group, Inc.
241 First Avenue North
Minneapolis, MN 55401 USA
1-800-4-KARBEN

Website address: www.karben.com

Library of Congress Cataloging-in-Publication Data

Names: Jules, Jacqueline, 1956– author. | Nayberg, Yevgenia, illustrator.
Title: Drop by drop : a story of Rabbi Akiva / by Jacqueline Jules ; illustrated by Yevgenia Nayberg.
Description: Minneapolis : Kar-Ben Publishing, [2017] | Summary: "With his wife's encouragement, a shepherd learns to read at age 40 and eventually becomes one of the greatest sages in Jewish history"—Provided by publisher.
Identifiers: LCCN 2016028352| ISBN 9781512420906 (lb : alk. paper) | ISBN 9781512420913 (pb : alk. paper)
Subjects: LCSH: Akiba ben Joseph, approximately 50-approximately 132—Juvenile fiction. | CYAC: Akiba ben Joseph, approximately 50-approximately 132—Fiction. | Rabbis—Fiction. | Perseverance (Ethics)—Fiction.
Classification: LCC PZ7.J92947 Dro 2017 | DDC [E]—dc23

LC record available at https://lccn.loc.gov/2016028352

Manufactured in the United States of America
1-41259-23234-11/14/2016

DROP BY DROP

A Story of **RABBI AKIVA**

Jacqueline Jules

ILLUSTRATED BY
Yevgenia Nayberg

KAR-BEN
PUBLISHING

Akiva came from a poor family. He did not know how to read. He did not know how to write. His family could not afford to send him to school. Instead, Akiva worked hard to earn his living. He became a shepherd, taking care of a wealthy man's sheep.

The wealthy man had a daughter named Rachel. She admired the gentle way Akiva tended her father's animals.

She watched as Akiva visited the sick and shared whatever he had with others in need.

Rachel loved Akiva. She knew that a man with such goodness in his heart, who understood so much about life, must be smart even if he did not know how to read or write.

One day Rachel told her father, "I am going to marry Akiva!"

Her father was shocked. "My daughter may not marry a shepherd! You should marry a rich, educated man. You deserve a large house, beautiful clothes, and fine food!"

"I would rather be Akiva's wife," said Rachel. "He is a good man. He works hard. And he has an excellent mind. Someday he could be a great scholar."

"A scholar? Him? How ridiculous!" her father exclaimed. "If you marry him, I will give you nothing. You will be as poor as he is."

Rachel married Akiva and they were indeed very poor. But they loved each other and made the most of what little they had.

After several years of living together in happiness, Rachel said to Akiva, "You know, my husband, you should study. I think you will enjoy learning."

"I am forty years old!" Akiva protested. "I don't even know the letters of the alphabet. Is it possible that I could start school now as if I were a young child?"

"Of course you can," Rachel said with determination. "Nothing is beyond you."

But Akiva doubted himself. "What if I can't learn? What if my brain is hard like a stone and can't absorb new ideas?"

"I believe in you," Rachel insisted.

Later that day, Akiva stopped by a brook so his sheep could rest and drink. Thirsty himself, he cupped his hands to gather water dripping down from one rock to another. As he drank, he noticed a hole in the bottom rock.

"Water is soft," Akiva thought with amazement. "And yet, drop by drop, it has managed to cut through this hard stone."

"My mind is not harder than a rock!
I can learn—just like water cuts
through stone—a little bit each day."

Though Akiva was a grown man, he sat in a classroom with young children. The children giggled behind their hands.

But Rachel comforted him. "Pay no attention to those who laugh. Work hard and you will succeed."

Akiva memorized the sound and shape
of each letter in the Hebrew alphabet.

He put the letters
together to form words.

Every day, he mastered a new word until he could read and write whole sentences.

Rachel beamed as she watched her husband read out loud in a confident, clear voice.

"It is time for you to study Torah, our Jewish history and law," Rachel said.

"But the school for such study is far away," Akiva said. "I would have to leave home."

"The best teachers are there," she said. "You must go. And you must stay until you have learned all that the school can teach you."

So Akiva left, promising to return.

Akiva was away for many years. He studied the laws of the Torah carefully one by one, just as he had learned each letter of the Hebrew alphabet. No word was too small for him to question or think about.

His teachers admired his wisdom and began to ask his opinion on important matters.

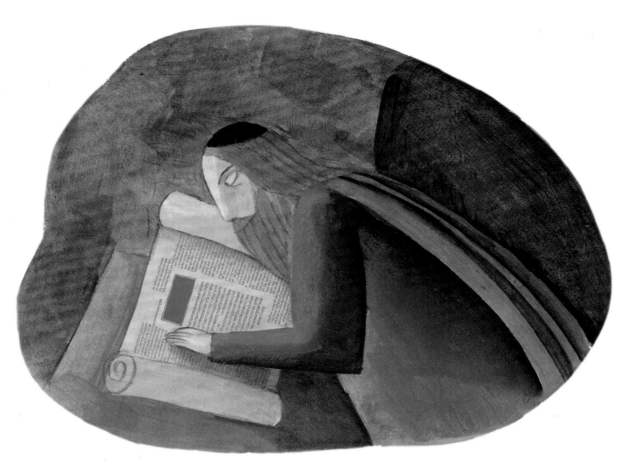

The man who could not read or write became
a wise rabbi followed by thousands of students.

All this time, Rachel waited, proud of her husband as she worked, saved, and planned for their future.

At last, Akiva returned home. When he reached his village, people streamed out of their houses to get a glimpse of the famous Rabbi Akiva.

Rachel had to push through crowds to get near her husband. As she drew closer, his students stepped in front of her.

"Do not bother Rabbi Akiva," said one student, not knowing who she was. "He is a very busy and important man."

"Wait!" cried Rabbi Akiva. "Do not turn this woman away. She should be standing right here beside me."

"This is Rachel, my wife," he told his students.
"She must share credit for my success as it
was she who believed in me before I knew a
single word of Torah. She understood before
I did that little by little, like water can carve
through stone, I could learn to read and study.
And little by little, I have proved her right!"

AUTHOR'S NOTE

Rabbi Akiva is considered to be one of the greatest sages in Jewish history. He became famous at the end of the first century. His example of learning to read at age 40 shows us that it is never too late to change our lives. But he could never have achieved what he did without his wife Rachel. She married Akiva against her father's wishes and spent years in poverty while Akiva studied. Rachel's sacrifice showed tremendous faith in her husband's abilities. She is a hero, too.